CHASING A DREAM

SUDHA DIXIT

COPYRIGHT @ 2022 CHASING A DREAM
By Sudha Dixit

Edited by Marie Ezekiel
Arranged by Tess Ritumalta
Illustration by Angelica Abundo

ISBN:
Hardbound-978-621-470-333-3
MOBI/KINDLE-978-621-470-334-0
Softbound/Paperback-978-621-470-335-7

Published by:
Poetry Planet Book Publishing House
Rosario, Pozorrubio, Pangasinan, Philippines
Contact Number: 09554960094
Email: maritesritumalta@gmail.com

DEDICATION

My children are my strength. They have supported me at every step, in life. They have set me free to do what I love to do without having to worry about running the house. Hence, this collection of my poems is dedicated to them – Richa, Rishi and Riju, the youngest and so matured. Love you children.

GRATITUDE

I am grateful to my brother Dr. K. P. Sharma (Vijay to me) for all the support, he provides me. I am grateful to Geetha Nair, a poet, story writer and a great human being who helped me putting together this book. Again I am thankful to Tess Marites Ritumalta for her love and care for me.

PREAMBLE

Chasing A Dream

We, all are solitary individuals. Some are lonely, some are not but every one is alone. I had been lonely. I lived in dreams. My Ivory tower was my library. Books provided me imagination. I developed a virtual wander lust. Poetry became my companion. All my hopes and aspirations have found place in my writing. Poetry proved a boon in fighting my loneliness. It never let me be morose and confined during Covid. My love for reading and writing kept me engaged throughout the lockdown period. I was able to get many of my books published during this time.

I am a dreamer; never stopped dreaming, even, in adverse circumstances. Hence this book is titled – "Chasing A Dream".

FOREWORD

And when they dare to tell you about all the things you cannot be, you smile and tell them, 'I am both war and woman, and you cannot stop me.'

These lines from "An Ode to Fearless Women" by Nikita Gill leap into my mind and linger there when I reflect on the poems of Sudha Dixit. The persona of her poems is one such woman whom the years cannot chain. She is a bold and passionate human being who does not drink life with coffee spoons but drains the cup to the lees. Her amazing zest for experience, her flights in the face of convention, her intense love for nature, her ability to find joy and comfort in little things are some of the themes that recur in the poems in this collection.

Sudha Dixit's poetry has similarities with that of the celebrated American poet, Emily Dickinson. Both do not experiment with form but write almost alway in quatrains. Both make much use of rhyme. But while Dickinson occasionally experiments with rhyme or casts it aside to suit her purpose, Sudha Dixit stays devoted to it. This is at times a constraint from which her thoughts and feelings strive to break free and fly high. Another common feature is simplicity of diction. The words used are clear; they shimmer like dewdrops on the grass. Sudha Dixit speaks directly and unequivocally to her readers.

There is much that this bold and zestful writer has to share with us.
"COLOURS OF LIFE" is a visually-appealing poem that ends with these lines:

I am glad that tears don't have colours in their
pains
Or else my face would have had many ugly stains.

One needs to keep these lines in mind when reading poems like this one, titled,

"HE LOVES ME"

I was cloistered and confined
Within the four walls
"You are safe and sheltered"
He said "That's all"

It was eerie
It was dark

Nothing to fill the void
All around shadows tall
Cobwebs of inhibitions
And
Customs' apparitions

Enmeshing imposed relations

Something, at my core, slugs me
Yet he says, he loves me

I am, now, no more
Of my older self
Just a haunted
Pathetic elf

But I should not complain and
Talk about what bugs me
For he says he loves me.

Yes; Brutus is an honourable man! What a poem it is! Though apparently simple, it holds within it the tears of countless generations. The poem captures the loss of freedom, lack of identity, the desolate plight of many an Indian wife.

In "HONESTY" a poem that holds the mirror up to her essence, Sudha Dixit writes:

Honesty is an introspection
One must look inside oneself
No façade, no masquerade
Truthfulness is self help.

The same theme finds expression in "SELF HELP" where she exhorts:

Let's break free from this cage
Let's drop this unreal mask
Let's live like actual couples
My love! Is it too much to ask?

Love is one of the poet's favourite themes and she writes about it with a rare candour and freshness. It is romantic love, a love that is doomed or cut short by death or parting that one sees in very many poems like "Sincerely Yours" ,"Lpve" and "A Love Poem."

 In a different vein are a few lines from "ROOTS":

My roots are my identity
My culture do they define
Sans them I am a non-entity
They are my life line.

They exemplify the importance Sudha Dixit attaches to her lineage, to what has through the centuries made her what she is today.
This does not mean, of course, that she accepts all that tradition has handed down to her. She battles fiercely against what she understands are meaningless mores and customs that stifle the individual and lead to a mechanical life. She writes in "NIGHTMARE":

A single step of steely nerve
Brings victory and cheers

The battles have brought her victory. "THE EMPRESS' is testimony to her serene self-confidence.

I am the queen in this brainy board game
I act and move at my own volition
I am the mightiest one in this creation.

This collection of poems is a clarion call to each one of us to have the courage to overcome obstacles in order to chase and capture our dreams. It shows us how to live and, in the final analysis, this is the grand function of poetry and of all art.

 I offer these lines from Sudha Dixit's poem "DREAMS–REVERIES" as a fitting conclusion to my attempt to capture the core of this amazing woman whom age cannot wither. This is the essence and the message of her compelling writing.

The eagle of my core's desire
Still flies so far and so high
It's not touched by time or age
Even now it reaches the sky

We survive through our dreams, let
Not our hopes and reveries ever die.

(Geetha Nair G)

TABLE OF CONTENTS

CHASING A DREAM

MY LOST LOVE

In laughter I found him
But lost him with tears
Since then, my life
Has gone out of gears

I presumed that from my mind
I have obliterated him
Till one day, in a crowded place
I, by chance, spotted him

All forgotten memories
Came rushing to surround me
I never knew that deep inside,
Still, they could hound me

High tide of recollections
Drowned me in a sea of woes
I realized that first love of life
From one's heart never out goes

Those recollections stashed in a cache
Keep surfacing again and again
Neither let me die of grief
Nor allow me to live in pain

Frankly, it's a jungle of reveries
With some flowers plus some thorns
Making me smile or tearful
Some adorn my mind; some make me forlorn

HONESTY

To judge our attitude
There's no weighing scale
Our own behavioural pattern
Gives signs which tell tales

When our friends do some wrong
Do we really point them out?
Do we give an honest opinion?
Or lie to show we're loyal and devout

Honesty is a virtue, revealed
In one's action character
If life is a book, it's there
In every page and chapter

Prior to pointing finger at others
If we look into the mirror
We'll know what's right or wrong
And will not make any error

Honesty is an introspection
One must look inside oneself
No façade, no masquerade
Truthfulness is self help

THE VACUUM INSIDE

It's I actually who am lonely
In this crowded city
In the quest of my love
I am being rather gritty
All around heat and dust
Not the world that was pretty
Why have I wandered out where
Earth's barren and sky empty
I've got, now, blisters on feet
I have lost my vivacity

DRIFTER

To maneuvers
The direction of movement
The broken oars fail,
Also, cannot follow the wind
With the tattered sails,
Hence my boat is simply drifting
Aimlessly, nowhere reaching
Similarly with delicate health
And the slow reflexes
I am taking life
As it comes,
Needs are less, expectations zero
My voyage my reverie sums
I was once a vivacious dreamer
Now, I am a resigned drifter

TWILIGHT

When the sun with bleeding heart
Paints the sky in vermilion hue
I feel sad and depressed, for
That's the time I remember you

With augmenting darkness
My sense of loneliness grows
I feel, in the whole world,
There is none, who my distress knows

Can sorrow be so beautiful
As displayed by twilight zone
It reflects unrequited love
With its bewitching euphoria gone

It's an artwork of nature
Showcasing fusion of emotions
Some feel joy and some see gloom
Yet it's magical without question

BEAUTY OF NATURE

The radiant sun
Travelled across the sky
In full glory,
Reached the edge of horizon
And fell into the
Abyss of darkness,
Leaving its light
Reflected
In the moon and stars
To keep the infinite
Space
Adorned in its absence.
So that, the
Beauty of nature would
Never die.
Swimming the dark ocean,
Fathoming
The depth of the
Bottomless abyss,
The sun would come out,
Again,
Tomorrow,
Brightening the universe,
With its golden rays.
I ponder over
The dark chasm of
My heart and
Grieve over
My unrequited love.
Some moments of happiness
Twinkle

Like the moon and stars
They nudge me
To be optimistic and
Strive for
A bright new start.
My core has
The depth
To think positively with
The strength
To scale
The vast space.
Life gives
A second chance
With a will and grit
We create a path
In life's journey,
To advance

MY HEART IS FULL OF JOY

My heart is full of joy
Emptied of negative thoughts
Reaching out to all
Responding with love-knots
Yodelling Xmas carols
Come, let us celebrate this day
Ring in the happy new year
Indulge in some fun and frolic
Sharing festivities with cheer
Thrill of decorating the tree
Magic of the gala moments
Anxiously, avidly waiting for
Santa and his bag of presents

PERFECT IMPERFECTION

I am a seeker of perfection
My role model is nature
Innumerable shapes and hues
It gives me a perfect picture

But can't define flawlessness
For, beauty has many facets
I've seen very tiny flowers
Also, big – petaled lotuses

Curly leaf, and twisted branch
All are, equally charming
Rippling lakes, gushing cascades and
Great waves, too, that look alarming

Winsome faced, fair complexioned
Woman of whom we often speak
How her charm is magnified,
Just put a black mole on her cheek

Imperfection which is unique
Gives a sense of true perfection
Singled out thing of beauty is
The divine spell of Creation

ALIENATED LOVE

You were kind and caring
Akin to generous shady tree
Liberal, lavish, unselfish,
Such luring qualities, I agree

But you weren't my destination
I could not stay with you
Rested under your cool canopy
It was a pleasure, that is true

My quest was something else
I had to quit and move on
Even when the sun was harsh
And, on the road, I was alone

Intense heat was so scorching
I got blisters on my feet
Yet, there was no turning back
I was beyond the point of retreat

Why! Oh why! That single memory
Keeps returning to my mind
Why are we living separate lives,
Wishing to retrieve what we left behind

Why should love have tragic ending
Why must it suffer isolation
Wall of misconception mars
Two loving souls' joy and passion

PRETENSE

We both know we are in love
But there is a discrepancy
You are much younger than me
And norms of society are fancy

When you're in love you know
That age does not matter
Even region, race, religion
Are such irrelevant factors

Thinking of what will people say
A secret rendezvous we've made
We cannot kiss on a dance floor
Outside as strangers we masquerade

We cannot leave each other alone
We yearn to live together
Then why do we live in pretense
As if we are friends not lovers

Let us break free from this cage
Let us drop this unreal mask
Let us live like actual couples
My love! Is it too much to ask?

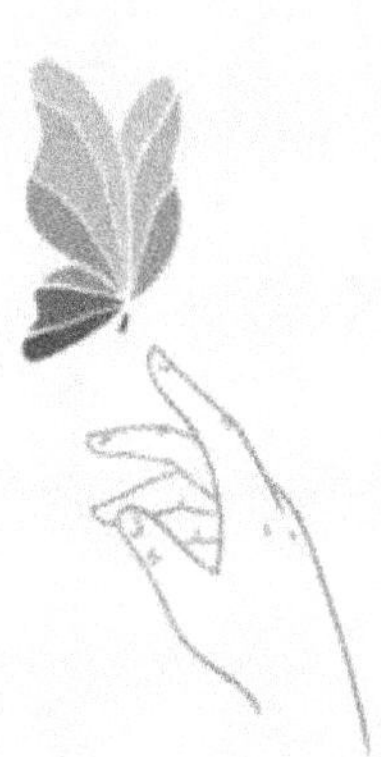

TOGETHER AGAIN

I looked at the path you took
While leaving me behind alone
My paradise seemed utterly lost
Whole universe looked forlorn

It's happy lush spring season
Full of colourful blooms
For me there's no celebration
Just an impending doom

I thought of you as an alchemist
Who would transform me into gold
But, now, I feel I am rusted
For being kept for long on hold

I'm incomplete without you
A cheerless lonely soul
If only I could get you back
That moment I'd be whole

Let's give it a try once more mate
Be friends sans lament and complaint
Let's forget vitriolic differences
And with love live together again

SERENDIPITY

I walked alone on a road
That was empty and desolate
I was not in a hurry to move fast
There was no one for me in wait

Suddenly, I heard my name
Someone had called me aloud
I thought it must be my soul mate
Who else, like that, would shout?

Yes! Someone claimed to be my friend
My happiness knew no boundary
But there were certain questions
Which put me in a quandary

He is a total stranger but
Seems to know me well
Whenever I hear his baritone
It puts me under its spell

But would it last, I wonder
Or is it my destination,
Have I found my love at last?
Or is it just a passing passion

A SECOND CHANCE

That time, not so long ago
I had fallen in love
Coming out of that euphoria
Was sorrowful and tough

Unrequited love makes one
A bit immune to romance
I, too, in my deep sadness
Forgot to sing and dance

But when, today, I saw you
My heart skipped a beat
I froze and kept staring
You were a visual treat

I felt weird and awkward
With a sense of déjà vu,
Stirred familiar feelings
The very sight of you

My heart is beating faster
Racing by leaps and bounds
My true love now for ever
Surely this time I've found

FOR YOU

I loved you, even, before we met
It wasn't love at first sight
I fell for your magical voice
It had filled me with supreme delight

A disembodied adoration
Blossomed into a devotion
Loved you despite your faults,
I harboured deep emotions

Do you know the purity of
The one-sided love mate!
Wish you to fall in love and
Perceive lover's mental state

Hope we're on the same wave length,
And feel the same sensation
Wrapped up in blissful ecstasy,
We reach the zenith of passion

My wishful thinking and
Reverie is only for you love
I get what I desire, even if
It is   extremely   tough

I know you will come to me, if
My faith in God is true
I always pray sincerely for
Divine gift that is only you

MEN WILL ALWAYS BE MEN

I do not think men are strong
They only look big and rough
I have seen them hiding their tears
It's a myth that men are tough

As beauty is only skin deep
Men's strength is a façade
They shiver in the face of crisis
Their bravery is just a charade

They lack a firm will power
On impulse, often, they act
A king-size ego is all they have
And that is a biblical fact

Their weakness is fair sex, till
Timbuktu they'd follow women,
Being incorrigibly romantic
These men always will be men

FATHER'S LOVE

My son! For nine months, your
Mother, kept you in her womb
I, too, have kept you in my heart,
Cherished you to grow and bloom

 My son! during gestation time
I felt you ever inside me,
I carried you in my heart
It'd nothing to do with anatomy

When I heard your first wail
My heart skipped a   beat
Moment, I realized its meaning
It turned into a melody sweet

You are still a little boy
Your mom looks after your needs
I am going to take care
Of all your actions and deeds

My son! You are my future
You'll be a better version of me
I'll try to be your best friend,
Mentor, father with bonhomie

Don't compare a father's love
With the love of your mother
Her feelings are celestial
I'm an earthly care taker

We   love   you with intensity
We   both   have similar   wish
Your   wellbeing and comfort
Is what we really cherish

MY PRECIOUS DATE

I wandered in lonely corridor
Looking for a companion
I needed a dance partner
For the college re – union,

By chance, a friend suggested
You, too, were on the lookout
Immediately, I knew you were
 The person, I was keen about

Though we were total strangers
Jointly   we glided to the dance floor,
Swirled and twirled with matching rhythm-
An experience I never had before

I know that you felt the same way
It was a heavenly dance
Slow music casting a spell
We both were in romantic trance

In that ceremony I found my
Keenly long-awaited soul mate
Love blossomed; our dream came true
Making that day my precious date

LETTING GO

I opened my treasure chest
Containing old memories
Some dried-up flowers
Several scented letters
And scribbled notes in diaries

The proof of betrayal
The sense of pain
A surge of anguish
Rushed all over me again
The box was full of miseries

I burnt all your letters and
Threw, old and dried up flowers,
Out of the window,
And tore down all
My dilapidated diaries

That contained your name, my beau,
I have wiped clean my slate
Of your distressing memories
Now, I am free from all anxieties
I've got rid of my naiveties

RELATIONSHIP

We were not related by blood
We had a special bond
I looked at him shyly with love
All he did was to respond

The chemistry was working
Developing   into   romance
We tied knot and formed a new
Relationship by design and chance

But the fate of love is despair
And   sorrow   of   separation,
Familiarity   breeds   contempt
Proximity   diminishes   passion

So, our alliance took a dip
His family did not like me
It   insulted, ridiculed and
With harsh words spiked me

Instead of standing by me
He succumbed to family pressure
I simply quit with a new wisdom
That blood is thicker than water

Now, I don't form relationships
I don't give love any tag or name
If my feelings are real and deep
I think I have attained my aim

A HAPPY CHANCE

I wanted to be left alone
I was in intense pain
Trying to hide my tears,
I came out in the rain

My anguish vanished when
I saw myriads of Hollyhocks
In awe I glanced around to find
Dancing   magnificent peacocks

My heart skipped a beat
At the sight of colourful blooms
And those charming regal birds
Made me forget my glooms
The sun peeped and came out
To intermingle with raindrops
Weaving a bright rainbow, before
It dipped down the hill – tops

Venturing   out to nature
Was for me a serendipity
I have found a magical trick to
Remain happy till eternity

WASTED LIFE

Oft for the glitter of wealth I yearned,
With perseverance and hard work, I earned
But after that a harsh lesson I learned,
That I cannot buy love for life I have burned

EVANESCENCE

A while ago
An echo
Then nothing
Just smoke
Smoke rising of
Dying fire
Of love's desire
Turning into
A ghost
The reason
The season
All got lost

WIND BENEATH MY WINGS

Under the harsh sun
On a treeless road
With blisters on
My feet I trod

Then suddenly I
Saw a cloud
Blocking the sunrays
Like a shroud

Struggling in rough sea and
The shore beyond my reach
A   big wave surged and
Tossed me on to the beach

There was a jungle fire
And I was caught in blaze
I know you rescued me
Though I was in a daze

You were always there
For me my divine Lord
With you as wind under my wings
Look, how far I have soared

On my life's canvas
Whatever picture I drew
Was due to your support
I'm nothing without you

FOR LOVE

I sing with the wind
I dance in the rain
Very thought of you
Alleviates my pain

How do I reach you love?
You live in far off land
In the jungle of my reverie
I wander like an eland

But one thing I know mate
We live in each other's heart
From this permanent abode
We're never going to part

I am a woman in love
For you I crave and pine
I'll go through the fire test
To make sure you are mine

Like a river to meet my ocean
I am always on the move
No hurdle can stop me
From reaching out to you, my love!

"RHYTHM"

It's a universal phenomenon
And it's visible everywhere
All elements of nature have it
Some awesome, some cute, some queer

Notice majestic cascade
Falling with a rhythmic roar
Spraying gleeful droplets
And displaying frosty hoar

Murmur of a flowing river,
Gurgling of bouncing stream,
Are a melodious rendition
Of songs with perfect rhythm

Even little babies react
To the musical beat
It's a gift of peace and joy
To the world – a cosmic treat

Be it a painting, dance or music,
All art forms have a rhythm
It's a feeling or sensation
Like refraction in a prism

MONEY

The most overrated thing
In the world, I guess, is money
It has its use along with blues
Like stings of the bees with honey

It's a necessary evil that often
Takes care of many needs
But obsessive love and craving for it
Spoils many   of our good deeds

Too involved in earning wealth
We forget, in our daily strife
That time has flown away and
We   forgot to   live our life

By diligence or by sheer chance
We   may get some prosperity
For peace of mind and contentment
We   need serendipity

Money can't buy everything in world
Moreover, lost wealth we can regain
But lost time is lost forever,
We pine and rue later —in vain

GIFT OF LOVE

I feel like Alice who fell in a pit,
And went to a magical wonderland,
I, too, fell but in love with you and
Reached a place I never planned

It was a terrain of sweet dreams,
A frenzied land of desires
Where first hint of romance I felt
And touched the passionate fires

This happened when by chance I
Looked in your eyes and disappeared
Detached from ground realities,
In the world of fantasy, I entered

Your eyes were the portal, where
I moved in and quickly vanished
Into exquisite Eden Garden, which
For me with love was furnished

Your laughing eyes invite me
To the dimly star- lit night sky
They whisper softly suggesting
Me to spread my wings and fly

The magic of your eyes inspires
A divine love in my heart
I dream and yearn without fear
It's your gift of a new start

REPUBLIC

Colour me, orange and yellow
With streaks of white and green,
Though I love all rainbow hues
Red, purple, and aquamarine

Our vibrant gardens cannot be
Dominated by a single shade
Forms of water also differ as
Flowing river, gushing cascade

Let our earth be green with flora
And saffron spread on sky
Let our pride be snow – white
Simple living and thinking high

Unity in diversity always
Being our culture's landmark
Equality and development
Should be kept in high regard

Let's plant trees or do something
Substantially different on this day
Leading from darkness to light
Celebrate our Republic Day

MY DAY OUT

It was my solo day out
But I was not alone
I carried with me dreams
And reveries high – flown

I etched my name on a cliff
I carved it on a tree trunk,
Laughed like a naughty child
With glee as if I was drunk

One day in such insane state
He saw me and smiled
His mocking eyes had me
Completely numb and beguiled

On cliffs and trees, together
We both put our signature
Love blossomed with our laughter
In the lap of wild nature

Those hills and those tree-trunks
Have our names till date
But angels of death came
 And I lost my soul mate

On my lonely day out
I walk alone once again
Sans dreams, reveries and laughter
I wander with anguish and pain

I forgot there were times
We used to press roses
In between the pages of a book
Songs, life, doesn't compose

A LOSS

I kept collecting grass and
Straw to make a nest
I wanted my abode,
In the world, to be the best
Ignored my ambitions and
Wish to reach the sky
Completely forgot that God
Has given me wings to fly

A CRAZY TRIP

I underwent a crazy trip
An adventure – an escapade
I came out unharmed from it, but
Its vivid memory doesn't fade

I visualized a forest
And unescorted ran away,
Really didn't know at what point
I went astray and lost my way

It was freezing, it was so cold
I was devastated that day
There was nothing to help me out
All I could do was only pray

Then I noticed a cottage well-lit
It seemed a God-sent sight
Someone up above cares for me
Who's always helping in my plight

I reached it, got food and shelter
In addition, a restful night
My friends, who were worried to death
At last found much needed respite

MODERN TIMES

I always thought my charming knight,
In shining armour, would come on a horse
I've been reading a lot of fairy tales, which
Filled my mind with myths of folk lores

But these are modern times alas!
We, now, live in the age of machines
Everyone is after material gain
Love has lost its romantic sheen

Natural, spiritual are, now, things of the past
Escalators, lifts and competition wars
Charm of horse-drawn chariot is gone
Romeos visit Juliets on bikes or in cars

Thrill of speed and madness of sound
Keep us where serenity has failed
I wish to turn the clock backward
And reach the era where peace prevails

SINCERELY YOURS

Do I really need to say?
Whatever all I feel for you
Just have a look into my eyes
Intense love, only, you will view

Still, if you really want to
See everything in black and white
I'll pick up a pen and paper
And a billet doux I would write

Have been waiting for years for you,
Hoping that you would come back soon,
Counting the twinkling stars at night,
I keep awake with lonely moon

Yes! I want to claim I love you
Only you are my life of course
You are in my heart forever
I am, my love, sincerely yours

COLOURS OF LIFE

All colours of nature in our life are reflected
Sometimes properly placed, sometimes deflected

Childhood had vibrant rainbow – hues depicted
Tender teenage, somehow, was pastel- shades addicted

With passage of time, life kept changing tints
Of many events and relations, it had umpteen prints

Then slowly and one by one, some colours left the
canvas
Losing all those dear one was a great loss alas!

Everything on earth is ephemeral by nature
Aging process, eventually, alters total pictures

Fag end of existence displays colours of cloud
Greyish white tinges hinting at an image of shroud

I am glad that tears don't have colours in their pains
Or else my face would have had many ugly stains

The canvas is blank, now, as all hues are gone
I, too, will be leaving soon on a journey all alone

DREAMS - REVERIES

Somewhat like my destiny
The sun is moving downwards
A tinge of sadness has crept in
The colours of life's canvas

The eagle of my core's desire
Still flies so far and so high
It's not touched by time or age
Even now it reaches the sky

We survive through our dreams, let
Not our hopes and reveries ever die

HE LOVES ME

He says he loves me
It must be true
If he says so
But
Suspicion casts
Its shadow
When I look back
My doubts grow

Was it love
When he made me quit
My studies
That were my passion
Was it love
When he forced me
To give up career
Which was
My ambition

He spoke
All this was hard work
He spoke
I need not bother
with such quirk

He did not ask my wish
He did not care to know
What I wanted to do and
What I really cherish

In fact, all this all miffs me
But he says he loves me

He made me slog with
So much menial chore
That made my heart ache,
That made my body sore

He does not even know
How much it hurts me
Cheekily He says that HE
Loves me

Freedom was totally denied
I was cloistered and confined
Within the four walls
"You are safe and sheltered"
He said "That's all"
It was eerie
It was dark
Nothing to fill the void
All around shadows tall
Also
Cobwebs of inhibitions
And
Customs' apparitions
Enmeshing imposed relations
Something, at my core, slugs me
Yet he says, he loves me

I am, now, no more
Of my older self
Just a haunted
Pathetic elf

But I should not complain and
Talk about what bugs me
For he says he loves me

25TH DECEMBER

This day is significant to me,
It's my sister's date of birth
She was my idol, my mentor
A source of joy and mirth

I never knew my biological mom
That did not make any difference
Didi took me under her wings
Like a mother in real sense

We would celebrate all festivals,
Complete with fun and frolic,
Life was a bed of roses with her
Not a single thorn or prick

I am not in proper mind – set
To celebrate this Christmas
My heart is heavy, my eyes tearful
I've lately lost my Santa Claus

LOVE

The Mango flowers are filling
My orchard with heady perfumes
Song birds have started singing
Their sweet melodious tunes

Spring spilling love in the air
Nature in its full fanfare
Beckoning and beseeching me to
Come out of my cloistered room

I dust off cobwebs of memory
Untangle myself from lethargy
To admire   Nature's beauty
Verdant leaves and colourful blooms

But something is sadly amiss
Your presence I strongly miss
The magic and euphoric bliss
Was you and only you I presume!

SYMBOL OF HOPE FOR HUMANITY

THE LAMP

Out of the vast variety
I have made my choice
A lamp symbolizes hope,
Makes humanity rejoice

It burns without respite
To keep our paths radiant
When sun goes down, the lamp
Shines, though not so brilliant

In a sombre blind tunnel,
In the total pitch darkness
A small flicker from a lamp
Dispenses with the helplessness

A good Samaritan – a wayfarer
Wherever it goes, spreads light
Underneath it there is darkness
It burns only for others' delight

It has inherent power to love,
Does not harbour love of power,
A symbol of hope for peace,
On thirsty earth, like shower

ONLY YOU FOR ME

The path of life's journey
Is full of ups and downs,
I often wear tiara of rose,
Sometimes, a thorny crown

Perpetual loneliness frequently
Causes my eyes to rain,
With grit and sheer will – power
I smile to hide my pain

And serendipity happened,
You came into my life,
I fell in love which meant
The end of my strife,

You filled the void I had
Deep inside the heart
But already you are planning
To leave me and depart

It's not going to be same again,
The magic would be lost,
In this life of desolation, you
Are the one I cherish most

I've only asked for you
In prayers each and every day
How can you desert me now
To go somewhere that's far away?

LONG DISTANT LOVE

Watching undulating waves,
Lying on a sandy beach
I crave for a possibility - if
You could be within my reach.

Then, in a flash, it occurred to me
That you might be thinking –
Perhaps I, too, am seeing the
Stars, which for you are blinking

The shining moon smiles
At me as well as at you,
All elements that divide us,
Can't diminish our love, it's true

I look at floating clouds and
Sense that somewhere far
It's raining in your region,
Nature's bliss keeps us at par

In the whole cosmos anywhere
Though we are in the distant parts
We are connected through,
Invisible strings of our hearts

We breathe the same air
We are under one sky,
To really meet sometimes,
We both crave and cry

HIDDEN TREASURE

Who opened my treasure chest
And left the lid ajar,
Confined from ages, now,
To get out, memories spar

Memories of unrequited love,
Memories of unshed tears,
Roses pressed in books secretly,
Memories of unfounded fears,

I had hidden them all in here,
Kept secure or so I thought,
Now they have come out of prison,
Exposing me as off- guard caught

Nostalgia is in the air,
Dried up wounds are re-opened,
Frozen pain, buried in my heart,
Has re-surfaced yet more deepened

I, now, need to close this box,
Contain these vagrant recollections
Must control my heartbeat,
That's racing with such reflections

CELEBRATION

It was just the beginning of
Less love and more distraction,
Then the final straw came when
I got his marriage invitation

Struck hard, it broke my heart,
I didn't know what to do,
Pulled myself up and decided to go
Treating the invite as a billet- doux.

I don't wear my heart on my sleeve
Always hiding my pain,
Smiling and laughing publicly,
I don't let my eyes rain.

I went to attend his wedding,
Offered him congratulation,
Nonchalantly I sang and danced,
Took part in full celebration

I knew I have lost him forever,
I walked back home alone
Steeled with grit and will power
Though feeling crumbled and forlorn,

None, in world, can put me down,
I am a woman of essence,
I don't need a knight in amour,
I am able to defy any offence

I'll live and find my real love,
Who'll love me for what I am,
Saved by God from someone, who
Brought me no honour only shame

Yes, I did go for his wedding, to
Show that I am done with him,
He'll not have the pleasure to know
That he could make me sad and grim

BORN FREE YET CAGED

Every human being's born free
But, everywhere finds himself chained
First in religion, caste and creed
Then for social norms maintained

Childhood is marked by discipline
Youth is bound by restrictions
Duties and responsibilities tie us
Often in our role selections

Twilight time sets us free
Only to a limited extent
With a diminished will to fly,
Living in a comfort zone and content

Door of the cage is opened, but
Our wings have lost the power
To soar all over the firmament,
Reflexes have become slower

Wish I had got this freedom earlier,
I could have scored the sky
Now, wobbling around the coop
I only crave that I could fly

A WISH

I wanted to put my head
 On your shoulder
And cry my heart out,
You kept avoiding meeting me,
On purpose no doubt,
You said you can't see me
In tears any time,
Yet, did not make me smile
For any reason or rhyme.
My tears have dried now,
I don't want to see you
Any time, I avow.

AN OCEAN

An ocean
I have kept
Hidden in my heart
Which contains
Pearls of wisdom,
Gems of desire
In a handsome
Treasure trove of art
Cool and collected
Serene and contented
Leading a sedentary life
No turmoil, no strife,
Living in an ivory tower
I was in a world apart
Suddenly,
As if a pebble one threw,
Rippled the surface
Of my sea
And the waves grew
Into tsunami with jump start
Sensation was amorous
A melody in a chorus
Tidal waves dancing on
My beaches out of focus
Obscured sense and reason
All I could just envision
Was a blinding blizzard
I need to know
Who caused
Upheaval in my heart
Who surreptitiously passed

By my silent region
In order to thwart
My hopeful vision
And without a backward glance
Managed to depart

MORE THAN LOVE

There are many more involvements,
Duties and obligations tough
We can't have only dreams and reveries,
And be content simply with love,

I wish to soar high in the sky,
I also have some goals to attain,
I have to leave you behind   my love
And go with a heart, full of pain

Though love has its own importance,
It fills up a void in the heart,
In the drama of our lives,
It does play a significant part

Yet love's not just earthly romance
It has a   boundless   connotation,
Spread all over the universe
It's to be shared with all relations

Your love isn't enough to bind me
I have to seek new avenue,
I know it would break our hearts
But with life we will continue

There are many more involvements
We must restrict our sentiments

LIFE

The journey of life is never ever smooth,
It's going to have so many ups and downs,
Sometimes we   get a garland of pretty flowers,
Sometimes we wear tiara of a thorny crown.

There are times when we soar high and fly,
Times – when we prefer to travel by a train,
At times we find it's a happy ride,
At times we wobble and walk in severe pain

Passing through an unlit dark tunnel,
Trekking   and stumbling in a dense forest,
Trudging   across the arid, sandy land,
Or scaling rocky, high mountain crests,

Whatsoever be the means or the time,
We must always move on and on,
With a caravan or with friends and if
There's no company, we then walk alone

We've to move with the flow of time,
For life's a journey without rest,
Life is soul's divine pilgrimage
In that supreme being's quest

CAVORTING

It's fun, it's frolic
It's see-saw like game
The bath becomes revelry
Though ritual is its name

Neither swimming nor skiing
It's, still, a sport
Pumping and spurting water
Happy kids cavort

We get pleasure in simple things
We cannot   buy happiness
Nature's treasure is bountiful
We forget all about stress

Can riches make us laugh
As does the child-like joy
Rapture has no parallel, while
Playing with, even, a broken toy

THE CHALLENGE

Tears are not going
To change my fate,
This bitter truth
I comprehended late,
Shadows will chase me
If I run,
I must turn
And let them
Squarely face me
There is no option
But to fight,
Must not cower
Or retreat,
To the Demon's
Delight
Let me hold back
My tears,
Take a deep breath,
I should take life head on
And defy Death

FROM MEMORY'S PAGE

Often in my younger days
Sitting on a sandy beach
Dancing with the sun's rays,
I saw, the rushing waves reach

To touch my feet as if to greet
My perennially pensive mood
As I strayed in the lost streets
Of my forgotten childhood

A happy time of climbing trees
Laughing, running with the breeze
Gleeful paper boat race
Exhilarating butterfly chase

Life's rainbow – coloured phase
Which I 'd never like to erase
Saved it all in my memory's page
Love being lost in the childhood maze

CHIMERA

You should have
Maintained that illusion
You were like fragrance
I couldn't have
Contained you
You were like breeze
I could not hold or have
 Imprisoned you
You were a dream –
A fancy
You were ethereal –
Fey and chancy
No way I could have
Confined you
For me
Only your being there was
My soul's vision
And reflection
You could have
Let me be
Under that delusion
Why did you
Have to break
That magic
That aura
That happy
Illusion

MY QUEST FOR ME

Wandering all alone in the
Dense forest of reveries
I encountered many apparitions,
Phantoms and the fairies

Am I searching for them, they asked
When I said "no", they vanished
Left alone, again, my valour and
My enthusiasm got diminished

At this juncture I changed my course
And ventured to the mountains,
Those hills gave me tranquility
With clouds, rainbows and rains

I was still not happy,
I went to lakes, rivers and seas
My quest remained unfulfilled,
I could not find peace

Desolate I sat in an arid desert
And looked inside my core,
Lo ! I was there within myself
I need not search 'Me' any more

A CARELESS LOVE

He was my man and he loved me, but
He was preoccupied with other things,
Always took me for granted and
Pulled me down by clipping my wings

Time that could've changed the fate of love,
He often spent in assessing my worth,
I liked to have fun and frolic in my life,
He confined me to the chores of home and hearth

Much later he realized the error
It was by then too late to mend
Disenchanted by his attitude,
I presumed he was not my friend

I accused him of exploiting
Me and my capabilities,
He laughed at me and denied
Saying he had responsibilities

He did regret, he had softened up
But he had, already, lost me
There was nothing left for him to
Win me back and accost me

THE LOVE BIRDS

Observing on a flowery branch
A pair of love birds,
A pang hits my heart
Listening to their chirps

In reality it seems
A perfectly beautiful sight
In normal circumstances
I should feel pure delight

I'm jealous of their love
For I am missing you
For no reason you left me,
I don't know what to do

I feel like screaming
Or hurling a stone
I want them to fly away
And leave me all alone

It's unfair on my part
But I am so morose
Why I always get thorns
While all others get a rose

ONCE IN A LIFE TIME

I have lived my life as I wished
On my own condition and term,
Anyone can verify this reality
Check on it and confirm,

That doesn't mean I have no regrets
In fact there are so many
I rue the fact that I didn't sin,
I've now got that epiphany

I can't turn the clock back now
I really missed those chances
I, too, had a beau but stalled
All his overtures and advances

It's okay to be pious and astute,
But at least once in a life time
One must taste the forbidden fruit
It's really not such a big crime

So much water has flown down the bridge
It will not be same, I know
I still hope against all hopes
I might, once more, find my beau

SEASON OF LOVE

Nature has been decked up as a bride.
On the clouds, with the wind, taking a ride

Verdant, new leaves have draped the bare trees
Singing in the rustling voice tickled by the breeze

When, in the afternoon, it rains with mild sprays
The sun also comes out with bright, gentle rays

They play a game of love at horizon high and low
And thus create a seemly, colourful rainbow

These symptoms indicate the spring in the air
It's season of intrigue, there's love in the air

The aura of excitement, the climate of romance,
A magical flavour spreads feeling of joyous trance

THE LAMP

Even before my birth, the soothsayer said
That I would be a guiding light,
That I would represent the sun,
In dark , by shining very bright

I didn't, at all, disappoint them,
Kept up the good work going,
To make the universe radiant,
I ever remained glowing

It was my pre-written destiny
With God's indelible stamp,
I'll have to go on burning, to light
Others' paths I'll have to be a lamp

MY ADVENTURE

Imprisoned, in this world, I was born,
Struggled for everything all alone
And remained in a desolate zone

But I had a very strong will,
Couldn't keep swallowing bitter pill,
So I planned to finish all those ills

Therefore I, first, broke the ties,
Transformed into a bird that flies,
Aspiring to reach the high skies

Then I went on a cleaning spree,
Swept the cobwebs, making mind free,
From a tiny seed I became a big tree

With my determination I changed the picture,
Life was throughout an adventure,
But ecstatically, I'm living in rapture

BARE NECESSITIES

I can live under a starry sky
I can manage with a grass skirt
But hunger is stark reality,
Lack of food does terribly hurt

We all have been born unequal
But, there are some basic needs,
Necessary for every being, to
Which we all should pay some heed

Costly clothes are not required, a
Roof overhead is shield enough
But children must not go hungry,
Life for them shouldn't be that tough

Children are future generation
They must have our care and protection

CAN SURVIVE ALONE

I live in a confined place,
Looking out of the barred door,
Let my imagination play
Which gives my poems wings to soar

I dream of the ocean,
With a sailing boat and breeze,
I think of pebbles and sea – shells,
Visualize both sands and trees

My body may not move out
But mind is completely free
On the wings of fancy, I can
Go out on a touring spree

My reveries are my strength,
They keep me in comfort zone,
No one can undermine me,
I can survive on my own

THE ENCHANTED FOREST

I walked and walked, got tired,
Badly in need of some rest,
I saw a pretty verdant space
And entered a dense forest

I went inside, immediately
Dropped off in a slumber,
All of a sudden – with start
I woke up among a clamour

I saw the trees talking,
Some making weird sounds
Some teetered and some wept,
None else was there around

A chill went up my spine,
I got an eerie feeling,
Not comprehending situation,
My head started reeling,

Then I realized that
The woods cannot walk,
So went to the crying trees,
To question them and talk

They told me they were thirsty,
That's irony of fate,
For trees create water, to this
Fact humans can't relate

The trees are being axed,
To gratify man's greed,
Jungles are disappearing,
Making space for city's need

I realized the horror of
Felling trees for selfish gains
Humanity would be extinct
With precious resources drained

NIGHTMARE

A recurring dream, from
Childhood haunts me,
The scary, shady figure,
Faintly visible, daunts me

I know it's a phantom from
My past, who's stalking me,
Giving me creeps at my
Vulnerability and mocking me.

In the darkness of night
Window pane shatters,
I get up with a start,
Listening   to clatters

Munch's "Scream" mingles
With   my cries,
The horror and the
Darkness   intensifies

I need to clear my head,
Drive away the poltergeist
I recall that with an angel,
Once, I had a tryst,

Who told me to think of
Happy moments, when worried,
It makes the demon of dread
Runaway scurried,

So, I gathered courage and
Looked straight in demon's eyes
It stopped, retreated and
Shrank down in size.

I made the ghost vanish,
No more nightmares,
A single step of steely nerve
Brings victory and cheers

NATURE

I love flowers and their colours
Red, blue, violet, pink, yellow,
I would go down to the garden,
Feel good and elated fellows

You should know what it does to me
Makes me happy and so blissful,
I was not so at ease before
Always   wanting, very needful

Nature is my guide and mentor
All joy I get is from her store,
I've less, want less, never greedy
Glad with what I have, want no more

A DRIFTING BOAT

I look beyond horizon, and
Wonder what is behind it
In search of whom the sun
Goes down in order to find it

He comes out in the morning
Smiling, bright and gleeful
Like one after spending night with
The beloved looking beautiful

I sail on undulating waves,
Feeling depressed and so lonely.
Clouds with rain, the breeze with scent
I feel a grudge, watching them fondly

I have put down my rickety oars,
I am at the mercy of high wind, see
My boat is drifting aimlessly
Just a vagabond which I'm destined to be

EARTH DAY

Does anyone know the pain,
A mother endures while giving birth,
Yet, never utters a woeful word
Only shows joy and spreads mirth

A naughty child, a cranky family
Test her grit and tolerance
But her acute sense of duty
Never fails her perseverance

Her hills denote her loftiness,
Oceans have depth of emotions
Her trees regulate the climate,
Winds are philanthropic notions

We take her goodness for granted,
We misbehave and injure her,
By cutting trees and blasting hills,
We make the whole humanity shudder

Our earth is the only planet, which
Has properties of a life giver,
Should be respected as a goddess,
For she is, simply, a mother figure

ENOUGH IS ENOUGH

Why I am tied tightly in chains,
Is it to increase my anguish and pains

I've always been bound by traditions
I dared not, ever, indulge in sedition

In this society patriarchy reigns
And against women bias it maintains

I accepted it all this sans any complaint
I've always been so meek and obedient

This bondage makes me sad and furious
I will defy this injustice and I am serious

Hell hath no fury as an angry lass
So I resolved to show them my real class

I tried and found the chains very fragile
And wondered why I waited all this while

Changing my aptitude and my style
I have become tough, I'm no more docile

WINGS

I want to have wings
And fly so high above
A nest somewhere on a tree
Yet in the sky an alcove
I want to be a symbol
Of world peace and love
With soft demeanour and beauty
I'd like to be a dove

AN ETHEREAL LOVE

I loved you with my heart,
It had nothing to do with body,
I never tried to capture you,
You were like fragrance or melody

For me you were a concept,
Spiritual form of love divine,
You did not comprehend that,
I had to draw a straight line

Leaving me you've gone away,
As a gust of blowing wind
You thought that you have freed yourself
But I have got you pinned
You are confined in my head,
With bunches of memories,
No longer in the melody of heart,
A prisoner in mind's stories

HESITATE

He was not very attractive
But I was drawn to him, with charm
Anyone he could captivate
I wanted him to approach me,
I wanted him to accost me
Reaching him, I would hesitate

Feminist and a modern girl
I'm equal to men but, at times
Girlish thoughts, mind dominate

Love makes you demure and feeble,
Less combative, also causes,
Romantic notions infiltrate

I can never make the first move
I'd like to be amply pampered,
Only then, love would culminate

While opening passion's flood gate
I'd always pause and hesitate,
Till I find my real soul mate

SPELLBOUND

In the quest of some inner peace
I went into the woods,
I needed to placate
My agitated mood

The fetching hues of leaves
Of brownish, verdant trees,
The colourful, wild flowers
Swaying in gentle breeze,

The melody of its silence
Spoke in surreal voice
No better place for a mood lift,
I found a nook to rejoice

So far from the crowd
In nature I have found
A magical beauty, which
Has kept me spellbound

THE LOSER

In the hustle bustle of life
I was destined to lose the game
I never made a clever move,
Was known as a pawn by name

Would it make a difference
If I were the mighty queen
She only serves the king
Defending him by all means

Sita was a royal princess,
A queen and loyal wife,
But lived as an exiled one
On the chess – board of life

The game of chess mirrors the world
With black and white pieces
There are some virtuous beings
And some are full of vices

Pardon me for I cannot play
This devious game of chess
There are some expert players
Who are thus really blessed

FAREWELL

Often you have gone away
Leaving me stranded,
Once again I'm sitting alone
Sifting sand and empty handed

What kind of relationship
Are we going to have,
If that is your attitude.
Or that's how you'd behave

A mystic moon, twinkling stars
Do not brighten my life
The vacuum you have left behind
Is filled with much strife

I, too, deserve some happiness
I wish bon voyage to you
I'm moving on, in life love !
So let me bid you adieu.

WITHOUT YOU

It was a breezy and sunny day
There was joy all the way,
I waited anxiously for you
Keeping all sad thoughts at bay

Moments turned into long hours,
There was no sign of you,
Your absence was not unusual
But for which I had no clue

All of a sudden the lights dimmed,
My world looked so dark,
The atmosphere of happiness
In a flash became stark

I perceived the flowers wilt,
I felt the lack of breeze
Sense of déjà vu cause my
Apprehension to increase

The aura of delight
Was there because of you
The beauty of surroundings
Always had you in view

You are the magic wand
Only you bring me my bliss,
And now without you,
My world is just an abyss

MOTHERHOOD

A lonely childhood
A meaningless marriage
Never known in life
An iota of happiness

But the woes and pains
That made my life sore
Disappeared the moment
My baby knocked at my core

I smiled and danced
I twirled and I pranced,
Picked up my cute kid and
With gay abandon danced

Unparalleled is the bliss of
A mother's joy in the world
Mere presence of her child
Makes all her sorrows blurred

GLACIER

There is a glacier
Inside me
A frozen river
That does not flow

No wonder
My heart has become
Hard as stone and
There is no spark to show

It requires some fire
To melt
Some tender care
Some warmth heart - felt
And lots of love
To be kept aglow

Don't know how long
It took to freeze
But it will take
some time to thaw
It has nothing to do
With attitude
It is simply
Nature's law

Come to me with
Warm demeanor
Touch me with your
Gentle hands

Make me gush with
Gay abandon
Make me alive with
Your love and Passion
Bring to me the melody
That my heart may sing
Transform this glacier
Into joyful spring

COFFEE

A happy memory,
A transition from
The days of lemon-drops
And toffee
To the bitter-sweet and
Aromatic coffee.
My first taste of
This brew was
In the misty,
Manipuri hills
Along with wintery
Fluid clouds
That memory
Still thrills
Amidst the throng of
Family and friends
As a lonely
Teenage girl
I stood at the edge of
The valley
With hot cup of coffee
In my hand, and
 Stared at its magic swirl
It contained some
Shadows of romance
And imaginary love
That put me in
A trance
 Now, after an eon
I am still fascinated
By that twirl,

It throws me back
In time
And drowns me
In a whirl
It's magic,
It's a sorcery,
It's not a brew
It's a memory,
My hot cup of coffee

DADDY'S ANGEL

I had made a solemn promise
To my partner, my sweet lady
I will fall in love second time
Only when I become a daddy

Now I hold my darling baby
Happily, in my blessed arms
I will do everything to protect
And keep her out of all harms

Wrapping her arms around me,
 To me she warmly clings
A fount of affection springs up
I kiss her brows and rosy cheeks

I, now, feel the ultimate,
Heavenly bliss and joy
Best gift that God has given me
Since I was a young boy

My gorgeous little angel
My life's greatest love
She's everything in world to me
My butterfly, my dove

For nine months, she was
Secure in the womb of her mom
And all that time I nursed her
In my mind with aplomb

Her entity is, we all know
Her mother's body's part
But this is also true, that
She is born in my heart

THE QUEST

Caught up in my wander lust
without   baggage, minus friends,
Set out on a journey through
A   dense forest
Only belongings that
My mind carries,
And fistful of memories
Filled in my treasure chest
An impulsive and
Impromptu jaunt
Towards a port of call unknown
All desires, all ideas, forgone
Except one burning thirst
To walk and walk without rest
Even with blisters on my feet
Till I see the gleam
The meaning of my dream
Signifying the end of my quest

ROOTS

I bloomed like a flower
I swayed with the rustling breeze
Danced on the tip of a thorn
And sang with murmuring trees

I laughed with gay abandon
Raised my arms to soar in mirth
Realization dawned on me
That I am rooted in the earth

At first, I felt dismay and woe
Then better sense prevailed
My roots were my protection
That logic was unveiled

I withstand mighty cyclones
I brave stormy tempest
My roots keep me safely bound
When I venture out in my quest

We all are often totally naive
And not at all street smart
We get enticed by outside pull
We fail to look inward

How can I disown my source?
How can I sever those ties?
The earth is my final destination
Even when I sour in skies

They bring for me the sap of life
From under the depth of earth
They suck out nutrient for me
And give me colour and mirth

My roots are my identity
My culture do they define
Sans them I am a non-entity
They are my life line

MY LIFE'S CANVAS

Holding my blank canvas
I looked around
To choose from the myriad hues,
Nature displayed.
Was the blue, I'd chosen, from the sea,
Or was it from sky
Maybe it was from my inside.
I had hidden the unfathomable
Ocean in my heart,
I contained the infinite
Sky inside me.
I wallowed in my blues
They've made me a recluse
I sit alone in pensive mood,
I cherish my solitude.

Sometimes I pick up the green
From verdant foliage
It's easy on the eyes
Gives me peaceful message
Red, violet, pink and yellow
Also come alive and bloom
My life, like my canvas
Does not have any gloom

THE HOMELESS

An unending line of distraught walkers
Moving towards an unknown location
Are children suddenly, rendered homeless
Follow a path with no destination

War wreaks havoc on the innocent lives
Random killings sans justifications
Thirsty, hungry and tear–stained sad faces
Lacking happy laughter and elation

Image of child, lying dead on a beach
Mother dragging children by feeble hands
Father carrying meagre belongings
Leading his family to no-man's lands

Fiddling gleefully, while Rome was burning
Who are these symbolic, evil Neros
Let's find out and eliminate them all
Politicians, who think they are heroes

MEMORY

Don't accuse me
Of being too busy
To remember you
Your memory is like
The air
Carrying oxygen
I keep inhaling.
Even when
I am busy or
Absolutely free
I remember you
All the time,
Thinking of you
Every moment
Just as I
Keep breathing

DREAMS

I keep gazing at the stars all night
Sleep is eluding me and I am sad
Send the dreams, with the next courier,
Which are left behind all those I had

Dreams have kept me forever going
Dreams have made me delighted always
They had done it in the long-lost past
And will still do even now for days

LOST & FOUND - ADD

I lost him in the
Wilderness of reverie
Wandering
Confused and lonely,
Tried to forget
And move on,
But,
He is still there
In my memory

Sudha Dixit

BEWARE

I am the chosen one,
My bleeding heart
May cry out
If you hurt me,
I may utter words
Which I don't want to
If you try to
Subvert me.
No one, ever,
Should care for you
If you don't me
Comfort me
Loneliness would be
Your destiny
If you are insensitive and
If you ever desert me
It's a cry of
Wounded core
It will cause you suffering
In case your actions
Disconcert and hurt me!

TIME

Like a perceptible wind
Imperceptibly it blows
Though invisible; yet like
A visible river, it flows

It moves only forward
No turning back it knows
The wind may change direction
Straight but, time goes

Still, it leaves on all of us
Its footprints permanently
The mirror shocks us, showing
Our face different completely

They say time and tide
Never wait for anyone,
Signs they leave behind,
Stay and can't be undone

We come and go eventually,
Time is omnipresent
Time is the only constant
Everything else is evanescent

THE PIANIST, MOONLIGHT SONATA & SPRING

My dreamy eyes see your shadow
In the eerie moonlit night,
I haven't come to terms with the fact
That you are far and not in sight

The cherished grand piano, which
Was your constant companion,
Looks forlorn and deserted, longing
For bygone days, craving for reunion

I still hear the melody you'd played
Under dimly – lit starry skies
With fingers dancing on that keyboard
Like fluttering flirting butterflies

There are tell-tale signs that
Spring is in the air,
Confirms the fragrant breeze and
Flowers bursting in colours

The night is so lonely and I
Miss your rendition my love
Sans you, your moonlight sonata
Does not bring me joy enough

It's a wishful thinking darling,
It may not have any logic,
You will come back to me,
To play for me magical music

MISS YOU MA

I lost her when I was very young,
How do I reminisce about her,
She is a vague and distant memory
There's nothing distinct that I remember

She is only a concept – just a notion divine,
A mere idea of an angelic being
Someone, who for a while, cared for me,
Even now, for me she is praying

Now, when I, myself am a mom
I know what a mother goes through
The children also reciprocate,
They respect and love you

Hence I perceive the emotions
I have for my offspring
I know that my mother also
Must have been loving and caring

As they say, God realized,
He couldn't be everywhere,
To designate his duties
He, then, created a mother

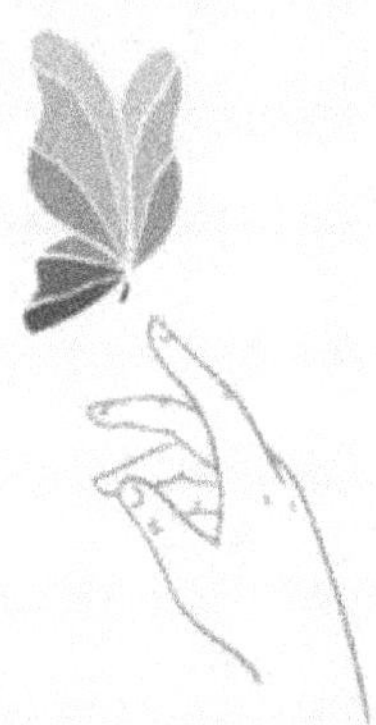

MY FRAGILE MESSENGER

How many nautical miles away
My love, you've gone today
Sans ship, steamer or boat,
To find you I can only pray

Stranded on a lonely shore
Raking my mind for a way
To send at least a message
I found an innovative play

Sometimes we put our hopes
On a feeble piece of hay
Distress, somehow, finds out,
In pitch dark, a shiny ray

I picked an ordinary paper,
And made a beautiful boat,
That was my billet- doux for you
I set it in the sea to float

Keeping my fingers crossed, I
Pleaded with my angel, my lord
To let my missive reach to you
For that was all I could afford

The faith can move a mountain
And I believe in God sublime
He is so kind and caring
He's there for me all the time

THE MIRROR ON THE WALL

"Mirror, mirror on the wall,
Who is the fairest of all"
Many times I heard the fable
When I was a little ga'l

But until the present day
I haven't got a reply
How can a mirror select a
Winner from, those who vie

Mirror has to tell the truth
That is his basic duty
It must reflect the fact
Be it ugly or beauty

I know I was a fair maiden
But that was ages back,
It shows a different face now
With wrinkled skin slack

I cannot blame the glass for
Letting me know the truth
And hinting that I am aging,
That I have lost my youth

But I'm not, only a body,
I am not, only a face,
I'm also a soul divine, I'm
Getting matured with grace

HAPPINESS

The dancing swan on the lake
Splashing water fascinates me
Reflection showing equal and
Opposite reaction also attracts me

I see my own image as a butterfly,
Flitting around from flower to flower
Also as peacock with its fanned out plumes
Prancing gloriously in rain shower

The laughter that's manifest
With gay abandon in any act
Is infectious as everyone who's
Touched by it is lit up in fact

A thing of beauty spreads cheer,
A positivity it brings
Joy reigns supreme in arts, when
One dances and one sings

MY EMOTIONS MY TREASURE

Have you seen sand
Slipping down your palm
Do you still
Feel unmoved and calm,
Seeping through your fingers
Solid or liquid –
Whatever, nothing lingers
Nothing stays more than
A few moments
Except the memory
That torments
Yet, I cling to that dream
Even though the pain
Makes me scream often
Maybe I am losing it
But
Whatever be the cost
Hanging on to the
Last straw
I'll save what
I cherish most
These emotions proffer me
An ultimate peace within
And create a masterpiece
That's for me
An award and
A rare win.

OUR PLANET

Hand in hand with dreams in the eyes
We hoped to live in joy and peace
What happened to those days my love,
Why all around troubles and worries

Our enchanted nature is facing
Ecological danger and threat everyday
We chop trees and blast the hills
Thus keep its splendour now at bay

Riots, murders, battles and rapes
Even children are not safe,
Where've the art and beauty gone
To music people are deaf

Sky is shouting loud and hoarse
The earth is shedding tears
The oceans fight stormy wind
The shores are living in fears

Humans are growing in numbers
Humanity is being extinct
To save planet we must recognize
The tell tale signs distinct

Unless we stop and think
There's threat of total annihilation
Love our earth, sky and oceans
Save our dreams by rumination

A SPARK IN MURK

It was like a dark tunnel
I groped around my way
There was zero visibility,
Destination was far away

There wasn't another option but
To have faith and keep going
I hoped that any moment I'd see
At least some stars glowing

It wasn't a mere experience
It wasn't a dreaded dream
It was the saga of life which
Was dark without a gleam

My faith was my strength,
I knew the murk would disappear
The tiny spark of optimism
Would make glum life happier

The sun cannot be stopped
It might be a lengthy night,
I continued to move ahead
At the tunnel's end I saw light

YOU ONLY LIVE ONCE

I am just a soul visiting human world
I am given a home here to dwell,
Built of five elements, just to fulfill
and perform duties through this cell

This is really my one and only chance
To prove all my significance and worth,
I must excel in the task for which
I'm sent in human body onto this earth

I may not have charm and good looks
I should, instead, be a good human being
Must lead an ethical, virtuous life,
Ostracize all the sinful and wrong doings

Simultaneously I should be enjoying this
Existence and worldly life to the hilt
Pleasure is a vital and an integral portion
Of the matters of which we are built

These diverse elements will disperse away
Once we attain our aim and divine goal,
We will then cease to live this life,
And become one with Supreme, ubiquitous Soul

THE CURTAIN

There was a drab curtain
With a painted grey cloud
The sombre colour made it
Look like a cheerless shroud

I wanted to unfold and see
The actual dramatic scene
So picked up central edge
Of fabric of the screen

I found all my fancies
My dreams hidden behind,
It was a vibrant world a
Beauty to which I was blind

We must open our eyes,
To see allure of nature,
Dust off the mirror of life,
Perceive its blissful rapture

We all are in the quest of
Ambrosia of love's wine
Which will unveil the secret
Of supreme soul divine.

DEAR DADDY

Since the time we declared
God created mother, for He
Couldn't ever be present in
The universe and everywhere

They feel they are "man" enough,
They can accomplish such a task
They've become better human beings
Than many of their counter parts

This denotes a welcome change,
Sharing of duties happily,
Brings home a serenity
And completes the family.

SUN IN MY PALM

Sometimes while walking
I pause and look back,
There were so many vicissitudes
In the life's track

A very lonely childhood,
A gypsy life style,
In a sea of tribulations
I was a solitary isle

I faced stormy winds
I fought the difficult time,
Some moments turned out bad
For no reason and rhyme

I am gifted with perseverance,
My faith moves mountain,
In adverse circumstances, too
My grit and courage I sustain

So I challenged the sun
That I will overpower him
Now I hold him in my palm
I look bright and he is dim.

NOT WITHOUT YOU

I keep awake whole night
I keep touching my cell phone
I don't want to miss your call
I'm all ears for the ring tone

I fancy you, I dream of you,
I wish that every moment
I should be there always, my love,
Wherever you are present

Your magical words stir me and
Make my heart beat faster,
Listening to your sophisticated talk
I feel I'm hearing the master

Your voice has a lyrical quality,
In it's melody I am lost
It's the kind of charismatic music
That I love and enjoy the most

Whatever you do, fascinates me
Wish to be a part of everything that's you
I don't want to live a moment, even
In paradise, if it is without you

BROKEN CONNECTION

My phone broke,
And along with it
My contact with him broke
This should not have happened
When we are in love,
A trivial accident like this
Should not much matter,
So, what if a little gadget
Got shattered,
Like old times
We could write love letters,
Which were so delightful
 With rhythms and rhymes
If everything fails,
We have the telepathy
With each other's plight
We have such empathy
Hence, phone or no phone
Our love is strong enough
We still dream together
When things are going tough

"THE CAGED ONE" OR "THE CAPTIVE"

I am a captive – in a cell,
Though it's pitch dark,
Some rays of light are filtering in
Through the bars

They symbolize hope,
Let me not be morose
Let me not lose heart
To a new dawn, I am close

So, come ! Lets talk about the unlimited sky
Lets talk and dream about the wish to fly

FACELESS

Always lonely and without love
I found solace in dreams, with
Faceless lovers and companions
As moving shadows in extremes

I would sing in soundless melody
With gay abandon merrily I dance,
In an imaginary close proximity,
Wrapped up in a blissful trance

No recognition, no attachment
Just to keep away the blues,
No betrayal, no jilted love, only
Me and my melodious muse

But, there burns a tiny flame
In my core, consuming all,
Dormant desire wants a name

MY ANGEL – MY MENTOR

I can't live with myself alone anymore
There's no one to give me company here
I need an escape; I wish to be lost
Take me beyond the moon dear

I may wander like a nimbus cloud
I'd like to shine resembling stars
Let raindrops hide my tears, besides
Washing away all my scars

I have ambitions, hopes and aspirations
I need some love and amity
Some angel must have sent you
 To me, like a serendipity

You're my guide, friend and philosopher
I'd learn about the world from you
I would follow you to the end of the globe
And emulate whatever things you do

Just help me to stand on my feet
Let me learn from the book of life
A little assistance from you my mentor
Would surely lessen the pain and strife

So let me be your follower
Impart your knowledge on me
I promise with my dedication,
I'll be wisdom's epitome

MAGIC

I had never believed in magic,
Now, I am a converted person,
I have seen the whole world change
And I have learned my lesson

All of a sudden there was beauty,
Tranquillity and joy in nature,
Flowers blooming, peacocks dancing,
Birds singing in divine rapture

Happiness reigns around and above
Since I'm under the spell of love

"ECSTASY"

I am in a blissful state
Aura of joy pervades me
I am a woman in love

I want to run in the garden,
Dance with breeze and feel
The warmth of joy in love

Euphoric under the clouds, I
Want to sing romantic songs
And shout out "I am in love"

I've broken all the shackles
Free of numerous inhibitions
I have found wings in love

LET'S BECOME STRANGERS AGAIN

So much water has flown under the bridge
Since we have been living together, so
Let's be strangers again and change the weather

They say that familiarity breeds contempt
Let's not fall into that rut
To while away the monotony
Let's take a stand that is clear cut

We should move on in life,
To explore some different avenues
Innumerable doors are open for us to
Colour drab life with myriad hues

So don't be sad and don't brood
Don't harbour thoughts that are morose
Let's learn to love the thorns that safeguard the
rose

CHARM

I saw them both together – one was fair and pretty
In stark contrast , the other one was dark and gritty

It was   hard to discern who was more winsome
The courageous, caring lass or the one as cute as
spectrum

I am a keen observer , I see intrinsic beauty
Not carried away by emotion, I do what I consider
duty

The beauty that is skin deep, does not appeal to
me
Only inner allure and goodness is charm's epitome

The acumen and resolve of the dusky one I choose
And ephemeral, enticing lure I always refuse

It's divinity and truthfulness that I consider charm
These are the sacred qualities which keep my heart
aglow & warm

THE EMPRESS

It was a game called chess
Of which I knew much less

They tried to treat me as a pawn,
And had, for me, some dictums drawn,

Asked me to move one step at a time
But to that diktat I didn't give a dime

I galloped two and half squares as a knight
And dared them to say that I wasn't right

I moved with aplomb like the forceful rook,
Flouted all rules that they wrote in their book

Didn't let them teach me to walk straight and obey
I wished and moved only diagonally - the slanting
way

By any standard I am no blue – blooded royalty,
But that is okay, for the king needs security

I am willful and better than all of them
I am the queen in this brainy board game

I act and move at my own volition
I am the mightiest one in this creation

SUMMER

The chill of wintry wind has gone away,
The fragrant summer breeze is nice and warm
The frost bites I got during the winter,
Are being soothed by the breeze applying balm

Bringing out the memory of school days,
A nostalgic sensation envelops me,
The clandestine tryst under mango tree
Leaves me, even today, with a weak knee

After the stressful period of exams
It used to be the time for vacations
And most of us go out for holidays
To the cool and coveted hill stations

Later we are unhappy with harsh summer
And go back to crave for the cool winter